SOLDIER'S PROTECTION

A SWEET MILITARY ROMANCE

HONOR VALLEY ROMANCES

SHANAE JOHNSON

THOSE JOHNSON GIRLS

CHAPTER ONE

Gabriel Thompson gazed out at the serene landscape of Honor Valley. With its peaceful atmosphere and picturesque scenery, it was the perfect place for him to focus on writing the non-fiction book he had envisioned since separating from the military. The book was a planned collection of stories about soldiers struggling with post-traumatic stress disorders who had successfully reintegrated back into their civilian life.

The weight of his own combat experiences was ever present on Gabe's broad shoulders as he took in a deep breath of fresh air. He had hoped that by sharing others' experiences, he could find relief and redemption for himself. Since he'd kept to himself while he was writing, he had no barometer to measure his progress with.

The wind whispered a gentle breeze, wafting through Gabe's short-cropped dark hair. His gaze scanned the mountains that loomed protectively over the valley. The cabin Gabe rented was an idyllic retreat nestled among tall pines on the outskirts of town. Cozy and rustic, with natural light streaming through its windows, it was perfect for a man like Gabe, who was accustomed to roughing it in the great outdoors and not yet ready for urban comforts. The scent of pine needles and wood smoke permeated the air, grounding him in nature's embrace.

Gabe sat at the modest wooden desk, his fingers hovering over the keys of his laptop as he struggled to find the right words for his manuscript. When his phone rang, he happily jerked his fingers away from the keys and reached for the device. Glancing at the screen, he winced at the name on the caller ID.

"Hey, Sally," he said, trying to sound upbeat, but the tension in his voice betrayed him.

"I just finished reading your third revision," said his editor without preamble, "and I have some concerns."

Gabe braced himself, gripping the phone tighter. "What's wrong?"

"Your writing is excellent, as always," Sally began. "But I think we need more personal stories from you. This book will resonate with readers if they can connect with you and your experiences."

Sharing his own experiences meant tearing open old wounds that Gabe wasn't quite ready to expose. "My story isn't really relevant here. I want to focus on helping others understand PTSD and how to support those suffering from it. I'm not in a relationship."

Gabe had no support. His parents had passed while he was in college. His last relationship hadn't lasted more than a couple of months in between deployments. He enjoyed his solitude and didn't have anyone he needed to make accommodations for.

"Healing comes from vulnerability," Sally was saying. "You need to bleed on the page."

He'd already bled on the battlefield. Wasn't that enough?

"If you want this book to succeed, you need to make it personal." Sally sighed. "Just think about it, okay? We're partners in this, and I want what's best for you and the book. I'll expect additional pages by the end of the month."

After hanging up, Gabe stared at the blank screen before him. The cursor blinked back mockingly. The weight of the conversation with Sally still hung heavily on Gabe's mind as he laced up his running shoes. He needed to clear his head, and a jog along the beach would do just that. Stepping out into the crisp air, Gabe took a deep breath, feeling the coolness fill his lungs.

Honor Valley was a picturesque small town, nestled between majestic mountains that cradled it like a protective embrace. As Gabe began his jog, he marveled at how the vibrant hues of the lakeside beach front seemed to dance against the backdrop of earthy, rustic homes. The town had a perfect balance of modern comforts and natural beauty, making it an ideal sanctuary for healing souls.

Gabe's focus was drawn to a commotion ahead. Two boys, both around ten years old, were engaged in a heated exchange by the side of the road. The smaller kid, fists balled and face red with anger, was hurling insults at the taller boy, who stood impassively, taking the verbal abuse without retaliating.

"Hey, string bean," the smaller kid yelled. "You think you're better than me? Just 'cause you're tall doesn't mean you're strong."

Gabe slowed to a stop, watching the scene unfold with concern. The bigger kid could easily push down his tormentor, but he remained steadfast, weathering the storm of words without fighting back.

"Come on, hit me. I dare you." the smaller kid taunted, shoving his finger into the taller boy's chest.

The taller kid did nothing, which surprised Gabe. When the little kid pulled back his fist, Gabe stepped in.

"Leave him alone," Gabe called out, his voice firm and authoritative. The smaller kid's head snapped in Gabe's direction, his eyes wide with surprise. The little kid ran off.

Gabe approached the taller kid, noting the quiet strength in his posture. "You okay?" he asked, crouching down to meet the boy's gaze.

"Yeah, I'm fine," he said.

"You're pretty tough not letting that get to you," Gabe said. "Why didn't you defend yourself against him, though? You could've easily taken him down."

"I don't believe in using violence against weaker opponents."

"That's a wise approach," Gabe said.

"My mom says that real strength comes from our character, not our fists."

"She sounds like a wise woman."

"She's the best." The kid's face lit up when he talked about his mother, revealing just how much she meant to him. "I gotta go."

The boy ran across the street, headed toward a diner. As he disappeared into the quaint establishment, Gabe noticed a book lying on the ground, forgotten amidst the commotion. Picking up the plastic-covered hardback, he realized it was a library book. He could simply return it to the library, but something inside Gabe urged him to return it to the boy himself.

CHAPTER TWO

Charlotte Evans balanced a tray of food on her arm as she weaved her way through the bustling diner. She wore a smile on her face that reached her warm brown eyes, despite the worry lines that tried to make their presence known. Joe's Diner was a cozy little spot nestled in the heart of a small town where everyone knew each other. The smell of freshly brewed coffee and sizzling bacon filled the air, accompanied by the gentle hum of laughter and conversation.

"Here you go, Mr. Kacee." Charlotte placed the plate in front of an elderly man with a kind face. "Eggs over easy, just how you like them."

"Thank you, Charlotte," he replied with a smile, dropping a few crumpled dollar bills onto the table as a tip. Charlotte picked up the money and pocketed it, hoping that the rest of her tips today would be enough to cover the overdue credit cards and an upcoming car note.

As she turned to head back to the kitchen, she glanced around the diner and caught sight of her reflection in the polished chrome napkin dispenser. Her long brown hair was pulled back into a no-nonsense ponytail. She smoothed down her apron, trying to ignore the pang of anxiety that surfaced as she thought about the mounting debts left behind by her ex-husband.

"Charlotte," Joe called out from behind the counter. "Order up for table four."

Charlotte turned from her harried reflection and hurried over to grab the food for table four. Her warm smile never faltered even as she navigated through the crowded space.

"Charlotte, you've really outdone yourself this time." Mrs. Jenkins took a bite of the indulgent chocolate cake that had become the talk of the town. "Your desserts are simply divine."

"Thank you, Mrs. Jenkins." Charlotte's cheeks flushed with modest pride. For her, baking was more than just a hobby; it was the one thing that brought her respite from the chaos of her life. And it wasn't just Mrs. Jenkins who thought so—everyone in town raved about Charlotte's desserts.

Charlotte's ultimate goal was to own a food truck where she could sell her mouthwatering creations. She could already picture it: the cheerful pastel exterior, the enticing aroma of freshly baked goods wafting through the air, and the line of eager customers waiting to savor her treats. It would be her ticket to financial freedom and a better life for her and Noah.

Speaking of her son, she spied him out the diner's window. Noah's backpack was slung over one shoulder, and his curly brown hair bounced with each step. The sight of her son never failed to bring a smile to her face, no matter how difficult things seemed.

"Hey, buddy," she called out, waving him over to the counter. "How was school today?"

"Good," he replied, taking a seat on one of the red vinyl stools. "We learned about butterflies and metamorphoses in science class. Let me show you."

Noah slid the pack off his shoulder. The zipper was gaping open. Instead of admonishing him about things falling out, Charlotte decided to let it slide. It was becoming rare to see a huge grin on her son's face since the divorce.

The grin dropped from Noah's face, and his eyes went wide with panic. "I can't find the book I borrowed from the library."

That was just what she needed. If students lost books, parents had to pay.

The door chime rang, announcing another customer. Charlotte's heart sank as she looked up to see her ex-husband standing in the doorway. The look on Tom's face told her he wasn't here for a friendly visit.

"Hey, Dad," Noah said quietly, his previous enthusiasm dampened by the sudden change in the atmosphere.

"Hey, kid," Tom replied, barely sparing his son a glance as his eyes narrowed on Charlotte. "We need to talk."

Charlotte took a deep breath and forced herself to meet his gaze. Tom looked like a stranger to her. She couldn't find one trace of the man she'd fallen in love with a decade ago. Perhaps he'd never existed.

"I'll be there in a minute," she said to him..

As Tom made his way to a booth in the back corner, Charlotte turned to Noah, her heart aching for her little boy. She could see the worry in his eyes.

"Sweetheart, why don't you go sit at our usual table and start your homework?" she suggested, giving him a gentle nudge toward a booth near the front window. "I'll be right there as soon as I finish speaking with your father, okay?"

"Okay, Mom," Noah said, sliding off the stool and heading to the designated spot. He glanced back at her once more before opening his backpack and pulling out a notebook.

Charlotte took another deep breath, steeling herself for the confrontation that was about to take place. She had faced Tom countless times before, and she knew that the only way to get through this was to stay strong—for herself and for Noah.

As they slid into their seats, Charlotte noticed how Tom's presence seemed to cast a shadow over the otherwise cheerful diner. They were the lucky ones, though. They could all leave. Charlotte was trapped. No matter how hard she tried, she could never escape the suffocating hold Tom had on her life.

"Tom, the debts... I'm doing everything I can to pay them off, but it feels like every time I make progress, you spend more money and put us right back where we started," Charlotte said, trying her best to keep her voice level and calm.

"Those debts are as much your responsibility as they are mine." Tom's voice was cold and dismissive. "Besides, I have friends in high places who can take care of things if need be. Sheriff Johnson owes me a favor or two."

"Darren might be your friend, but that doesn't mean he can magically erase our debts. Besides, I don't want to rely on favors. I want to get out of this mess so I can finally start living my life."

"Your life? You mean chasing some stupid dream of owning a food truck?" Tom scoffed, rolling his eyes. "You should be grateful for what you have, Charlotte. Some people would kill for a steady job and a roof over their head."

Charlotte clenched her fists under the table, swallowing her anger and hurt. She knew arguing with Tom would only make things worse, and she couldn't risk that—not with Noah so close by. There was nothing more for her to say, so she got up from the table.

Tom gripped her hand. His fingers crushed hers with a force that made her wince. She glanced down at her wrist and saw the angry red marks where his nails dug into her skin.

"Look at me when I'm talking to you," Tom growled through gritted teeth.

Charlotte felt her heart pounding in her chest as she slowly raised her gaze to meet his icy stare. Inhaling deeply, she tried to steady herself, believing that if she remained calm, it might help defuse the situation. But every fiber of her being trembled with fear, and she couldn't shake the feeling that things were about to take a turn for the worse.

Charlotte caught Noah's eyes from across the diner. The worry etched on his young face brought a pang of guilt to her heart. She knew she had to reassure him.

Forcing a smile on her lips, she mouthed the words *I'm okay* to her son.

"Tom, please," she whispered, her voice trembling.

For a moment, Tom seemed to consider her words, his grip on her hand finally loosening. But as he looked over at Noah, his expression hardened once more, and Charlotte knew that their battle was far from over.

Just as Tom was about to say something else, the bell above the door chimed, breaking the tense silence. Both Tom and Charlotte turned their heads toward the sound, surprised by the sudden noise. The sun illuminated a tall and handsome man in his early thirties entering the diner.

Charlotte's heart skipped a beat as she took in the sight of the newcomer. He had short-cropped dark hair, a strong build, and a confident stride that seemed out of place in the diner where mostly the elderly were regulars.

The stranger turned his head as if he'd heard her thoughts. When his gaze landed on hers, Charlotte was brought back to the time when she was a child and she and her next-door neighbor played the game of telephone. They'd tossed a rope between their bedroom windows, attaching plastic cups to either end. But they'd never heard one another clearly.

Without his lips moving, Charlotte felt she heard this man loud and clear. His eyes asked if she was okay. She almost answered with the truth. That was until Tom stood up beside her.

Charlotte glanced back at Tom, who was watching the exchange with a mixture of annoyance and suspicion. For once, she didn't feel completely powerless under his gaze—instead, the presence of the newcomer gave her an influx of inner strength.

"Excuse me," Charlotte said to Tom, her voice firm. "I need to go take care of my customer."

Tom hesitated for a moment, clearly displeased by her sudden assertiveness. Before he could protest, Charlotte had already slipped away from the booth, leaving him behind as she made her way toward the handsome stranger.

CHAPTER THREE

Gabe approached the quaint little diner, his running shoes crunching on the gravel underfoot as he neared the entrance. Through the window, he spotted the familiar face of the boy who had been struggling with a bully's taunts earlier that day. The kid sat tensely in one of the red vinyl booths, gripping his silverware with white knuckles but remaining in place.

Gabe pushed open the diner door, and a sudden waft of cool air hit his skin, a welcome reprieve from the summer heat outside. The familiar scents of coffee and bacon filled the air, mingling with the sound of sizzling on the grill. He stepped inside the cozy diner, taking in its nostalgic charm—red vinyl booths lining the walls and a vintage jukebox standing proudly in the corner.

As he looked around, Gabe's gaze instinctively followed the kid's line of sight, landing on a woman whose beauty made Gabe's heart skip a beat. Even from across the room, Gabe felt an inexplicable connection to her. Her long brown hair was queued in a holder that allowed it to cascade down her back. She had the same eyes as the boy; dull at the edges with a spot of brightness at the center. She must be the kid's mother. The boy's eyes remained fixed on his mother as he continued to clutch his silverware tightly.

Just as Gabe was about to take a step toward her, a tall, imposing man moved into his line of view, effectively blocking any further glimpses of her. His menacing aura immediately put Gabe on high alert, his instincts honed from years of military service kicking in. Even though he didn't know this man, something deep within Gabe warned that he could be trouble.

Gabe exhaled slowly, trying to calm the storm of emotions swirling inside him. He knew he couldn't interfere directly—not yet, anyway—but he couldn't stand by and do nothing while this man terrorized a woman and her child.

Instead of approaching the woman, Gabe turned his attention from the man to the boy. The kid was clutching his cutlery tightly as if the knife and fork were a lifeline. Clearly, this was an all too familiar scene for the young pacifist.

"Hey there," Gabe said gently, crouching down to the kid's level. "I think you dropped this outside." He held out the tattered copy of *The Metamorphosis of Butterflies.*

The boy looked up at him, startled. Then his expression softened into one of gratitude. "Thanks," he said quietly. "That's my library book. I thought I lost it."

"I'm Gabe."

"Noah."

"Quite an interesting subject," Gabe remarked, sliding into the seat across from the youngster. "Do you like learning about butterflies?"

Noah nodded vigorously, his eyes lighting up. "Yeah, I do. Did you know that they go through four different stages before becoming butterflies? It's called metamorphosis."

"Metamorphosis, huh?" Gabe echoed, smiling at the boy's enthusiasm. "Sounds like quite a journey.

And a good lesson too—sometimes we need to go through changes and challenges to become stronger and better versions of ourselves."

"Mom, look. Mr. Gabe found my book."

Gabe hesitated to look over his shoulder. Because he could feel the warmth of her before he saw her. Turning around confirmed it.

She stood there, illuminated by the warm afternoon light filtering through the windows. The faint smile that tugged her lips was more of a solemn line, as though she had seen tough days yet refused to give in. Gabe had known war and violence, and he knew the kind of strength it took to smile through pain. It was etched in her eyes, mirrored in his own.

She had the kind of beauty that made a man want to dive in, to discover what made her laugh, what brought tears to her eyes, and what made her heart race. To Gabriel, who was born a writer, she was like a piece of classic literature, one he desired to unravel, understand, and cherish.

The dark shadow of a man loomed over her. Gabe felt a protective instinct surge within him. The man must have seen the threat in Gabe's eyes because he turned and walked out the door.

"Hi there," she said, her voice warm and

friendly. "I'm Charlotte, Noah's mom. I just wanted to thank you for returning his book. If he'd lost it, I would've had to pay for it."

She offered her hand to Gabe, who shook it gently, feeling an unexpected spark pass between them. He could see her gasp slightly, clearly feeling the same jolt.

"Gabe Thompson. Nice to meet you, Charlotte," he replied, still holding her hand for a moment longer than necessary before letting go. "It was no trouble, really. Just glad I could help."

"Please let me buy you dinner as a thank you," Charlotte insisted, her eyes shining with gratitude.

"Thank you, but I don't want to impose." Gabe's gaze lingered on her lovely face. "How about this? I'll come back for lunch tomorrow, when I'm not so sweaty from working out and can present myself better."

Charlotte smiled, her eyes twinkling with amusement. "Deal," she agreed.

With a goodbye wave to Noah, Gabe stepped out of the diner, the door closing behind him with a soft jingle. For a moment, he allowed himself to bask in the afterglow of his encounter with Charlotte and Noah, feeling cautiously optimistic about the connection they had formed.

"Hey, you!" a gruff voice called out, yanking Gabe out of his reverie.

He turned to find the man who had stood over Charlotte standing just a few feet away, his imposing figure casting a long shadow under the afternoon light. The anger radiating from him was palpable, and Gabe braced himself for the confrontation.

"Stay away from my family," he warned, jabbing a finger at Gabe's chest. His eyes darted between Gabe and the diner window where Charlotte and Noah sat.

"Your family?" Gabe asked, raising an eyebrow.

Could this man be Noah's father? He couldn't see the resemblance. Noah was the spitting image of his mother, and this man couldn't hold a candle to the light that radiated from both of them. But perhaps he had been the cause of the dimness at the edges of each of their irises.

"I saw the way you looked at her. You think you can just waltz in here and take what's mine?"

Gabe clenched his jaw, holding back the urge to remind this loser that people were not possessions. Instead, he maintained eye contact and said calmly, "I have no intention of causing any trouble. I was just helping out a kid who dropped his book."

The other man scoffed, unconvinced by Gabe's explanation. The tension between them built as their eyes remained locked, each man sizing up the other.

"Next time, drop the book at the library," the other man warned before turning on his heel and stomping toward the parking lot.

Gabe watched him go. That should have been enough of a warning. But Gabe didn't always take the hint. He knew that getting involved with Charlotte and Noah wouldn't be easy, but something deep inside told him it was worth fighting for. And as he walked away from the diner, he vowed to do everything in his power to protect and support them, no matter what obstacles lay ahead.

CHAPTER FOUR

Charlotte stood in the small, cozy kitchen of the diner, delicately folding whipped cream into a bowl of silky chocolate mousse. The scent of sugar and cocoa filled the air, mingling with the warm aroma of freshly baked pastries that lined the display case near the front door. She reveled in the precision of baking, finding the exact measurements and the knowledge that if she simply followed the recipe, things would come out exactly the way she wanted them to.

As she spread the mousse over a layer of moist chocolate cake, Charlotte wished that the rest of her life mirrored the predictability and control she found in baking. With each spatula stroke, a sense of calm washed over her, momentarily silencing the worries that often plagued her thoughts. Her love for her son, her determination to protect him, and the courage she showed in facing adversity were her guiding lights. But sometimes the weight of it all felt like too much to bear.

She thought of the man she'd met yesterday. She thought of the calm that had swept over her when he'd come into the diner. He was strong, kind-hearted, and there was something about him, an almost tangible air of resilience and hope, that made her want to be around him more.

"Focus, Charlotte," she whispered to herself, smoothing the final layer of mousse onto the cake. "One step at a time."

As she slid the dessert into the refrigerator to set, Charlotte took a deep breath and straightened her apron. Life might not be as predictable as baking, but maybe, just maybe, everything would turn out all right in the end.

The diner was bustling with activity as Charlotte's regular customers streamed in, filling the air with laughter and friendly chatter. The scent of freshly baked treats and bacon wafted through the room, mingling with the aroma of strong coffee. As she moved behind the counter, her warm smile never faltered, even as she juggled multiple orders.

"Charlotte!" called out Mrs. Naveen, a kind-faced woman in her sixties who frequented the diner almost daily. "I'm having a party next weekend, and I was wondering if you could cater it for me?"

"Of course, Mrs. Naveen," replied Charlotte enthusiastically, her eyes sparkling at the prospect of the extra income. It would be a nice boost to her bank account and food truck fund. "I'd be more than happy to help."

The bell above the door chimed again, announcing another customer. Charlotte looked up to see Gabe walking in. Her heart skipped a beat as she took in his appearance. Oh, but the man did clean up nice.

Today he was dressed in a crisp button-up shirt and dark jeans. He looked every bit the soldier she expected him to be. Honor Valley was home to a base, and most men who didn't grow up here hailed from there. Gabe carried a sleek laptop under his arm, raising a curious eyebrow as he approached the counter.

"Hey there, Charlotte," he greeted her warmly. "Just like I promised, I've come for lunch."

"Hi, Gabe. You look... really nice today," she

stammered, suddenly feeling self-conscious in her flour-dusted apron.

"I had a meeting this morning, so I thought I'd dress up a bit."

"Meeting?" She hadn't taken the time to consider the details of his life.

"Nothing too exciting," he assured her, setting his laptop on the counter. "Just catching up with an old buddy from my unit."

Charlotte gestured toward an empty booth. "Why don't you have a seat? I'll bring you our special for the day."

"Sounds perfect," Gabe replied and made his way to the booth. As he settled in, he opened his laptop and began tapping away at the keys.

Gathering a plate of steaming food, Charlotte walked over to his table and set it down in front of him. "Here you go," she said, trying to sound casual as she glanced at his screen. "What are you working on?"

"It's a book I've been writing," he revealed, pausing his typing to look up at her. "It's about soldiers dealing with PTSD and trying to find their way back to normalcy."

"That sounds really important." Charlotte's

respect for Gabe grew even more. "I bet it'll help a lot of people."

"Hopefully." He smiled, looking almost bashful.

As Charlotte refilled Gabe's coffee cup, she noticed the way he smiled at her. It was a smile that seemed to reach right into her heart, warming her from the inside out. She returned it, feeling a flutter of happiness that had been missing for far too long.

"Thank you," Gabe said softly, his eyes lingering on hers for a moment before glancing back down at his computer screen. "You know, I've been thinking about Noah's dad."

Charlotte froze. Despite the warm pot of coffee in her hands, her fingers went numb. "Did he say anything to you?" She hesitated as Gabe narrowed his eyes at her. "Did he… do anything to you?"

"No," Gabe said softly. "He didn't lay a finger on me."

Charlotte hadn't said the words. Tom had held on to her, leaving bruises. But he'd never struck her. Still, she had to look away from Gabe. She felt those piercing eyes of his would see that much.

"It's not just people who served in the military who suffer from trauma. Do you think he might be suffering from PTSD?"

The question caught Charlotte off guard. She hesitated for a moment. She had never considered that possibility, always assuming that Tom's anger was just part of who he was.

"No, I don't think so," she finally replied, shaking her head as she clung to her belief in Tom's inherent goodness. "Tom's just...he's always been quick-tempered. It's just part of his personality."

Gabe looked up at her with concern, his brow furrowed as he considered her words. "Charlotte, PTSD can manifest in many different ways, including anger and aggression. It doesn't mean he's a bad person; it just means he's struggling with something beyond his control."

"Maybe," she conceded, her voice barely above a whisper as she tried to wrap her mind around the idea.

Gabe reached across the table, gently touching her hand. Charlotte fought to not pull her hand away. The last thing she wanted Gabe to see was her bruises from the other day. But she knew that he'd seen them. Even more, his touch made the remaining aches fade away.

"I understand that it's hard to accept, especially when you've been through so much with him. But sometimes, understanding the root of the problem can be the first step toward healing."

Charlotte looked down at their joined hands, her heart aching for the man who had once been her everything. She knew that Gabe was trying to help, but it was difficult to let go of the anger and resentment that had built up over the years from Tom's abuse.

"Thank you, Gabe," she murmured, squeezing his hand in gratitude. "I'll think about what you said."

He gave her hand one last reassuring squeeze before letting go, returning his attention to his computer screen.

Charlotte busied herself with wiping down the countertop, trying to shake off the heavy emotions that had surfaced during their conversation about Tom. She glanced over at Gabe from time to time. He was steadily typing away on his computer. His plate of food was cleared. Charlotte decided to bring him a new plate. This time, it was filled with the dessert she'd made.

Gabe looked up at her approach. "I didn't order this."

"It's on the house. For helping with Noah. I made it."

He didn't protest as she thought he would. He picked up the fork, dug into the rich flour, and placed it in his mouth. His eyes closed, and he made a sound of ecstasy.

Charlotte looked around the near empty diner, her cheeks going pink.

"I feel like you're Eve. I've been handed an apple. And I'm well on the path toward sin."

Charlotte giggled. She stood by mutely as Gabe finished off the cake. When he was done, he set the fork down and looked up at her.

"Do you want more?" she asked.

His gaze roamed over her. It wasn't predatory. His eyes were filled with appreciation. "I think I've had enough for today. But I'll be back tomorrow."

Again, Charlotte stood by as Gabe gathered up his things. When he had everything in hand, he faced her once more. With a reassuring smile, he bade her farewell. Then he was out the door.

Charlotte watched Gabe walk away, her hand lightly touching her heart as he made his way across the street. The invisible chains of her past, her mountainous debt, the weight of her responsibilities, they all seemed a little lighter at the prospect of seeing Gabe again.

CHAPTER FIVE

The coffee shop was cozy and dimly lit. Gabe inhaled the rich aroma of freshly brewed coffee and warm pastries. The atmosphere was far more relaxed than that of Joe's diner. Aria, the owner of Sandy Perk, was a beautiful woman with kind eyes, but she didn't hold a candle to Charlotte. The soft chatter of conversations filled the air as Gabe pulled out a chair and sat down among his fellow veterans in the local PTSD support group meeting.

"Welcome, everyone," the group leader began. Faith was an older woman with a quick smile and a booming voice. Her eyes were at once compassionate and piercing, letting anyone who came under her gaze know that they were heard and could tell her more. "Let's start by going around the room and sharing a little bit about ourselves and our experiences."

As the others took turns sharing their stories, Gabe listened intently, feeling a tentative sense of camaraderie with these men and women who had faced similar traumas. A young woman spoke up, her voice trembling slightly as she recounted her harrowing time overseas.

"During my last tour, I lost two of my closest friends. It's still hard for me to accept they're gone. But being here, with all of you, it helps–" She paused, swallowing back tears. "It helps me feel less alone."

"Hi, I'm Terry," a man with salt-and-pepper hair spoke up, breaking the ice. "I was in the Marines, and I struggled with nightmares after returning home. But being here has helped me find some peace."

One by one, the other members of the group introduced themselves and shared pieces of their stories. When it came to his turn to speak, Gabe's hands clenched tightly in his lap as his throat tightened.

"Gabe?" Faith turned those piercing eyes on him. "Would you like to share something with us?"

Gabe hesitated for a moment, then cleared his throat. "I'm Gabe, former Special Forces," he started, his voice steady but tinged with emotion. "I've seen things and done things that still haunt me. But lately, I've been trying to focus on the good in my life."

There was a silent beat as the others waited for Gabe to fill in the blanks. Gabe gave a nod of his head as if to punctuate the end of his brief diatribe. He expected pushback but got none. Faith blinked slowly, but Gabe still felt that laser of her gaze on him.

"Thank you for sharing, Gabe," she said. "It's important to recognize the positive aspects of our lives even when we're struggling."

As the meeting wrapped up, Gabe covertly made his way to the door. He'd never been the most sociable of men, most often preferring to read books than make conversation. He hurried out because he wanted to capture the essence of the conversations he'd heard tonight.

There was so much richness he could add to his book after bearing witness to the trials and triumphs of those in the group. He knew he could successfully weave their tails into his narrative and make the book stronger and provide a greater depth of experience for other soldiers and families who faced what they all went through.

Gabe sat down at his laptop, feeling lighter than he had in months. As he began to write, the words flowed like a river breaking through a dam—overwhelming and cathartic. But he didn't find that he wrote about the stories just shared with him in the group. He wrote about his experiences in the military, the friends he had lost, and the nightmares that still plagued him.

The next morning, the sun's rays painted the sky in soft hues of pink and orange as it rose over the cabin. Gabe sat on the front porch of his small rental home, a steaming cup of coffee by his side, and his computer open on his lap. The words he had written—raw and unfiltered—stared back at him, acting as both a testament to his pain and a beacon of hope for the future.

As Gabe was lost in thought, the sound of laughter caught his attention. He looked up just in time to see Noah walking down the sidewalk, a book clutched tightly in his hands.

"Hey, caterpillar-face," a familiar voice taunted from behind Noah. Gabe's brow furrowed as he recognized the bully from before, a smirk plastered across the small kid's face.

"You know, Madison, everyone is like a caterpillar," said Noah. "We all have the chance to grow and change into something beautiful, like a butterfly."

"You're a dummy," Madison sneered before shoving Noah, sending both him and his precious book sprawling into the mud.

The kid ran away before Gabe reached the edge of the porch.

"Are you okay, buddy?" Gabe asked gently, helping Noah to his feet and brushing the mud from his clothes.

"Y-yeah," Noah sniffed, trying to hold back his tears. "But my book is ruined."

"Hey, it's just a little mud," Gabe reassured him, picking up the soggy tome and wiping it off as best he could. "We'll clean it up when we get inside, okay?"

"Okay," Noah agreed, his lower lip still trembling.

"Listen, Noah," Gabe began, kneeling down to be at eye level with the young boy. "Sometimes, people are going to be mean to you, and it's important to stand up for yourself. But there's a difference between defending yourself and being aggressive."

"I don't want to be like him," Noah said, wiping his tear-streaked face with the back of his hand.

Gabe didn't have to ask who the *him* was. He knew it wasn't Madison. Gabe clenched his teeth as he sucked in a deep lungful of air. He released the breath through his mouth, which softened his lips when he spoke again.

"Defending yourself means standing your ground and not letting anyone hurt you or make you feel bad about yourself. Being aggressive means trying to hurt someone else on purpose," Gabe explained, watching as understanding dawned in Noah's eyes.

"So I should only fight back if I really need to?" Noah questioned, his voice small but steady.

"Exactly," Gabe replied with a nod. "And I can teach you some ways to do that without hurting anyone."

"My mom won't like it."

"I'll talk to her."

After cleaning up his book, Gabe and Noah walked side by side, making their way to the small-town diner where Charlotte worked. The sound of clinking dishes filled the air when they stepped into Joe's Diner. There were far fewer people here than had been in Sandy Perk last night, but there was also a sense of community in the elderly folks eating their early suppers.

"Hey, Mom," Noah called out as he spotted Charlotte behind the counter, her long brown hair pulled back into a neat ponytail.

"Hey, sweetie!" Charlotte replied, her face lighting up at the sight of her son. But her joy quickly turned to concern when she noticed a neglected spot of mud on his face. "What happened?"

Noah bit his lip.

Gabe spoke up. "Noah, why don't you go and wash that off in the bathroom while I talk with your mom."

Charlotte looked to her retreating son, then to Gabe, then back to the bathroom door swinging closed.

"I think it might be a good idea to teach Noah some self-defense."

"Self-defense?" Charlotte questioned, her eyebrows knitting together in concern. "Did he get into a fight?"

"Not exactly. But the fight keeps coming to him."

Charlotte furrowed her brow in confusion, but she leaned in and listened to Gabe.

"Self-defense isn't about teaching Noah to be violent. It's about giving him the tools and confidence to protect himself when he's faced with a difficult situation. I want to help Noah learn how to stand up for himself without resorting to aggression."

Charlotte took a moment to consider his words, her eyes searching Gabe's face for sincerity. She seemed to be weighing the risks against the potential benefits.

"How can I trust that you're not teaching him to hurt other kids?" she asked, her eyes filled with both hope and fear.

"I promise you that I will only teach Noah how to defend himself if it's absolutely necessary—if he's alone and facing someone bigger and stronger than him." He reached out to touch her arm gently, the warmth of her skin beneath his fingertips anchoring him in the moment. "I'm trained to protect and defend, not to harm or provoke."

Gabe could see the wheels turning in Charlotte's mind, the indecision giving way to a cautious optimism. The sun filtered through the diner's windows, casting a warm glow on her face and illuminating the flecks of gold in her brown eyes.

Charlotte studied him for a long moment, as if trying to peer into his soul. "Okay," she agreed, albeit hesitantly. "We'll give it a try."

CHAPTER SIX

Charlotte stood on the porch of Gabe's small cabin. Her arms were crossed over her chest. She yanked them down to her sides, having come to learn in Gabe's teachings that that was a defensive posture. A soft smile played on her lips as she watched Gabe train Noah in self-defense.

"Okay, buddy, always remember to keep your hands up and protect your face," Gabe instructed Noah, who nodded eagerly. The boy's eyes were wide with admiration. He had become his teacher and his friend.

Charlotte's eyes were wide as well, but for another reason. She couldn't help but admire Gabe's physical appearance and fitness as he worked with her son. His broad shoulders flexed under his T-shirt as he showed Noah how to throw a punch, and his muscular legs moved with ease and agility.

"Mom, look at this," Noah called out to her, beaming with pride as he managed to block one of Gabe's gentle strikes.

"Great job, Noah."

Charlotte knew it was important for her son to learn how to defend himself, especially given their current situation with Tom. But more than that, she was grateful for the bond forming between Gabe and Noah, a connection that seemed to fill a void in both of their lives.

As she continued to watch them, Charlotte felt a warmth spreading through her chest, a feeling she hadn't experienced in a long time. There was something about Gabe that made her feel safe, cared for, and understood. And it wasn't just his impressive physical strength or his military background; it was the compassion that shone in his eyes, the genuine concern for her and Noah that he expressed through both words and actions.

"Come on, Charlotte," Gabe called to her, extending a hand. "Why don't you give it a try?"

"Me?" she asked, raising an eyebrow in surprise.

Under his patient guidance, Charlotte learned how to throw a punch, block a strike, and even take down an opponent—something she never imagined she'd be able to do.

"Okay, Charlotte, for this next exercise, I want you to act like an attacker, and I'll show Noah how to escape from your hold," Gabe instructed, his voice steady and confident.

Taking a deep breath, Charlotte nodded and approached Gabe, pretending to wrap her arms around him in an aggressive manner. He guided her into position. She felt her heart race as their bodies pressed together.

"All right, Noah," Gabe began, addressing her son while maintaining eye contact with Charlotte, "when someone tries to hold you like this, the first thing you want to do is create some space." With that, Gabe showed Noah how to use his elbow to push against her arms, effectively loosening her grip.

"Then," he continued, "you want to twist your body and slip out of their hold, just like this."

Gabe demonstrated the move, his breath warm on Charlotte's neck as he nimbly escaped her grasp and stepped away. But not before she felt the muscles of his chest pressed against her back. She tried to focus on his words instead of the way her heart raced at their closeness.

"First, stomp your foot down hard on your attacker's instep. This will cause them pain and distract them," Gabe instructed. Charlotte followed his guidance, trying not to think about how sturdy and immovable he felt beneath her.

"Good, now use that distraction to twist out of their grip and grab one of their arms," he continued, releasing her just enough for her to practice the maneuver. She spun around in his embrace, adrenaline pumping through her veins, and gripped his arm tightly.

"Perfect," Gabe praised, his eyes shining with approval. "Next, use your other hand to push against their shoulder while pulling their arm toward you. This will throw them off balance."

Taking a deep breath, Charlotte did as he instructed, feeling a surge of power as Gabe willingly toppled backward onto the soft grass below them. In an instant, she found herself straddling him, looking down into his surprised yet impressed expression.

Heat spread through Charlotte's veins as she looked down at Gabe, pinned beneath her on the sun-warmed grass. His broad chest rose and fell with each breath, his intense eyes filled with a mixture of surprise and admiration. She felt a ripple of triumph echo through her, her pulse quickening in response to the position they found themselves in.

As her shaky breath brushed over his face, she noticed the way his eyes flickered with something more than just surprise. It was a glimmer of desire, restrained yet there just the same. His arms relaxed at his sides, showing no intention to take control of the situation. He was submitting to her, and it wasn't out of weakness. It was a sign of trust.

"See, you're a natural," Gabe told her, his voice filled with pride.

"Can I try again?" Noah interrupted, reminding them of his presence.

Suddenly aware of their close proximity, Charlotte quickly got off Gabe, her cheeks flaming. As Gabe rose gracefully to his feet, their eyes locked again. An unspoken understanding passed between them, sparking an anticipation that made her heart race. The moment ended, but the connection did not. It was a beginning—the beginning of something she desperately wanted to explore. And from the look in Gabe's eyes, he felt it too.

Charlotte's phone buzzed in her pocket, pulling

her focus away from the scene before her. Noticing the call had gone to voicemail, she hesitated for a moment before deciding to listen to the message. The sound of Tom's voice began to fill her ears, starting off sweet and almost tender.

"Hey, Charlotte," he said softly, "I just wanted to talk to you about something important. I've been thinking a lot about us lately, and—"

His tone suddenly shifted, becoming darker and more menacing. "But then I heard you've been getting cozy with some guy in town. You really think I wouldn't find out? You're my wife, Charlotte. You belong to me!"

Her heart raced as Tom's threats continued, each word dripping with venom and control. The fear she had been keeping at bay threatened to envelop her once more.

"Charlotte, is everything okay?" Gabe asked.

"Mom, who was that?" Noah asked, his voice shaking slightly as he looked up at her with wide, frightened eyes.

"Sweetie, it's okay," Charlotte reassured him, trying to hide her own terror. But it was a lie. It was no longer okay. And for the first time in a long time, Charlotte was determined to do something about it.

CHAPTER SEVEN

The warm glow of the precinct's fluorescent lights did little to ease the tension that coiled in Gabe's chest as he stood beside Charlotte, his fingers flexing at his sides. He felt the weight of his past experiences bearing down on him, his protective instincts surging forward like a tidal wave.

"Sheriff Johnson," Gabe began, his voice low and steady, "we have reason to believe Tom Evans is becoming increasingly dangerous."

The sheriff looked like a former football star who had let himself go. His beer belly pressed against the buttons of his uniform. His face had the red marks that came from eating an excess of greasy foods.

"Tom Evans is currently out of town on a business trip," the sheriff said to Charlotte.

"How do you know this?" Gabe asked.

"I know," the man swung an annoyed gaze to him, "because I saw him off earlier this morning. And what business it is of yours?"

"It's my business when any man manhandles a woman one day and leaves a threatening voice message the next."

"Manhandles? Let me see."

Charlotte hesitated. With a look at Gabe, she held out her wrists.

Sheriff Johnson glanced down at her wrists where the bruise that her ex-husband had given her was fading. "You sure that's not a grease burn?"

Charlotte bit at the inside of her lip. She cast her gaze down. Her body swayed toward Gabe. Gabe placed a hand at her low back, hoping to infuse his strength into this strong woman.

"Play him the voice message."

Her fingers trembled as she pulled her cell phone from her pocket. The sheriff took the phone from her and pressed it to his ear. It was clear the man tried to keep his expression bland, but Gabe caught the twitching of his left eyelid and the slight purse of his lip.

In the end, he handed the phone back to Charlotte with a shake of his head. "There's no tangible threat there."

Gabe clenched his jaw, his thoughts racing. It was infuriating to be met with such indifference from the very people who were supposed to protect them. He knew all too well how quickly situations could escalate, and he wasn't about to let that happen on his watch.

"Sheriff, this isn't just about suspicions," Gabe said. "Tom is using financial abuse to maintain power over her. He's manipulative and abusive, and it's only a matter of time before he does something even worse."

Sheriff Johnson's gaze locked on to Gabe, a mixture of skepticism and hostility evident in his glare. "Tom Evans has been a respected member of this community for years. He's got a temper, sure, but I've never known him to actually hurt anyone."

"Maybe you don't know your friend as well as you think you do," Gabe shot back, bristling at the sheriff's dismissive attitude. He glanced at Charlotte, noting her downcast eyes and trembling hands. Anger surged through him, fueled by a desire to protect those who couldn't defend themselves. But right now, all he cared about was ensuring Charlotte's safety. "Understand this; I won't let anything happen to Charlotte or Noah. If you can't protect them, I will."

With a final, steely glance at the sheriff, Gabe guided Charlotte out of the police station. He knew that their fight for justice had only just begun. He vowed to himself that he would not rest until Tom Evans was held accountable for his actions.

"Thank you, Gabe," Charlotte whispered, squeezing his hand.

Stepping outside into the sun was such a stark contrast from the darkness they were facing. They walked down the steps of the precinct together, still holding hands, and stopped beside the row of flowering dogwood trees that lined the sidewalk.

"It's going to be okay, I promise." Gabe wasn't a man to make promises he couldn't keep.

"Right now, I'm just... tired," Charlotte admitted, her voice quivering slightly.

Her vulnerability touched something within Gabe, making him want to hold her close and shield her from the world. And so he did. He wrapped his arms around her.

When she returned the embrace, he tightened his hold. The air between them crackled with electricity. Gabe was acutely aware of every point where their bodies touched. He looked down at her lips—soft, pink, and inviting—and felt an irresistible urge to kiss her.

"Charlotte," he murmured, leaning in, drawn like a moth to a flame. Their breaths mingled, and he felt the warmth of her skin against his. Just as their lips were about to meet, a shrill ringtone sliced through the charged silence.

Startled, they sprang apart, their hearts racing for entirely different reasons now. Charlotte fumbled to retrieve her phone from her purse, an apologetic look on her face.

"Sorry," she said, her cheeks flushed with embarrassment as she answered the call. "Hello?"

Gabe watched her intently, his emotions a whirlwind of confusion and desire. He tried to push away the lingering taste of what might have been, focusing instead on the task ahead. They had a battle to fight, and he would do everything in his power to ensure victory for Charlotte and Noah.

Charlotte's voice wavered as she held the phone to her ear. Her free hand gripped Gabe's tightly. He instinctively moved closer, offering silent support. He wanted to snatch the phone away and tell Tom Evans exactly what he thought of him.

"Noah did what?" Charlotte said.

"Who is it?" Gabe inquired, his mind racing with possibilities—all of them still leading back to Tom.

"It's Principal Richards from Noah's school," she whispered to him. She bit her lip, clearly troubled by the information she was receiving. "I'll be right there," she assured the principal, ending the call with a shaky exhale.

Gabe's anger dissipated as quickly as it had flared up, replaced by worry. "What happened? Is Noah all right?"

Charlotte looked up at Gabe, her eyes filled with anxiety. "He got into a fight at school. They sent him to the principal's office."

"Is he hurt?" Gabe asked, his own concerns mirrored in her gaze.

"I don't know. I need to go to the school and find out." Her voice trembled, and he could see her struggling to hold back tears.

As they drove through the picturesque streets of their small town, Gabe couldn't help but notice the stark contrast between the idyllic scenery and the storm brewing in their lives. The charming storefronts and tree-lined sidewalks seemed almost mocking in their tranquility, as if they were taunting him with the knowledge that even in such a perfect place, darkness could still take root.

With their hands intertwined, they stepped out of the truck and made their way to the school's entrance, ready to face whatever challenges awaited them within.

The moment they crossed the threshold into the school, Gabe's mind raced with worry. He couldn't shake the nagging feeling that Noah's fight was somehow his fault. Had he inadvertently encouraged the boy to stand up for himself too aggressively? He recalled their conversation about self-defense and the demonstration of a few simple moves. The memory gnawed at him as they approached the principal's office.

CHAPTER EIGHT

harlotte strode into Principal Richards' office, her heart pounding as she gripped Gabe's hand tightly. The secretary, Mrs. Muhammad, glanced at them over her reading glasses, her gaze stopping at their intertwined fingers.

"Mrs. Evans?" Mrs. Muhammad said with a hint of surprise in her voice.

Charlotte looked down and realized she was still holding Gabe's hand. A blush crept up her cheeks, but she didn't let go. She needed his support now more than ever, especially when it came to matters involving her son.

"Principal Richards will be ready in just a moment. She's still speaking with the other parents."

On the other side of the room, she saw Noah. A quick glance showed that he was unharmed, but in low spirits. He was seated on a bench, flanked by two boys with bruises marring their faces. The sight made her think of her ex-husband—the man who had caused her so much pain. Had her sweet, gentle son become a bully like his father?

She felt her grip on Gabe's hand loosen as her mind raced with thoughts. After all, it was Gabe who had taught Noah how to fight. They had never thought that Noah would use those skills against others in this way.

Noah hesitated, his gaze darting between Charlotte and Gabe. Just as he opened his mouth to speak, Principal Richards appeared in the doorway. Two other parents walked out. Charlotte vaguely recognized them. They didn't meet her gaze.

"Mrs. Evans, please come inside," said the principal.

"Go ahead, Charlotte," Gabe encouraged, giving her a reassuring smile. "I'll stay here with Noah."

Inside Principal Richards' office, Charlotte smoothed her skirt as she sat down. The afternoon sun cast long shadows through the blinds, creating a somber atmosphere. Helen Richards folded her hands on the desk, her expression serious yet compassionate.

"Mrs. Evans," she began, "I want to assure you that Noah is not in any trouble. In fact, he showed remarkable restraint and maturity today."

Relief unclenched Charlotte's fingers. But she remained silent, waiting for the principal to continue.

"Two boys were picking on a smaller student during recess. Noah stepped in and stopped them from escalating the situation. He stood up for the other child and managed to prevent any further harm."

Tears welled up in Charlotte's eyes. She knew she had to give credit where it was due. Gabe had taught Noah not just how to defend himself, but also the importance of standing up for others.

"Your son has a good heart, Mrs. Evans," Principal Richards added, smiling warmly. "You should be very proud."

"Thank you, Principal Richards," Charlotte replied, wiping away her tears. "I am."

As she exited the office, Charlotte saw her son chatting animatedly with Gabe, their bond evident in the easy way they interacted. As soon as Noah spotted his mother, he rushed over to her, concern etched on his young face.

"Mom, I'm so sorry," he blurted out. "I didn't mean to get into trouble."

"Hey," Charlotte said gently, pulling him into a hug. "I'm not mad at you, sweetheart. Principal Richards told me what happened, and I'm so proud of you for standing up for that other child."

"Really?" Noah asked, sniffling and looking up at her hopefully.

"Really," she confirmed, smoothing his hair back from his forehead.

As the three of them walked away from the school, a gentle breeze stirred the leaves around them. Charlotte glanced over at Gabe, who was deep in conversation with Noah about their next self-defense class. Noah was asking if they might invite some other kids over to join in.

"Hey, Gabe," she called out, interrupting their chat. Both Gabe and Noah looked up at her expectantly, and she continued, "Why don't you come over for a movie tonight? We can pick something fun to watch together."

Gabe hesitated a moment, his eyes searching hers before he finally agreed. "I'd like that," he said softly, a hint of a smile playing at the corners of his lips.

"Awesome!" Noah exclaimed, bouncing on his toes in excitement. "Can we watch an action movie, Mom?"

Later that evening, Charlotte's living room was bathed in the soft, flickering light from the television screen as the opening credits of the chosen action film filled the room with a dramatic score. Charlotte sat on the couch, snuggled under a cozy blanket and a bowl of freshly popped popcorn on her lap. On either side of her, Gabe and Noah were similarly settled, their eyes glued to the screen.

"Thanks again for coming over, Gabe," Charlotte said quietly, careful not to disturb Noah's focus on the movie.

"Thank you for inviting me," Gabe replied, his voice equally hushed. Their eyes met briefly, and Charlotte felt her cheeks grow warm. She quickly turned her attention back to the movie, a flurry of thoughts and emotions racing through her mind.

As they watched the film together, Charlotte found herself acutely aware of Gabe's presence beside her. The scent of his aftershave wafted over to her with every subtle movement he made, and she had to resist the urge to snuggle closer to him. She knew that there was something special between them, something worth exploring.

Despite the action unfolding on the screen, Noah's eyelids were growing heavy as sleep began to claim him. His head lolled gently against Gabe's shoulder. Charlotte smiled at the sight of her son, so content in the presence of the man she was beginning to fall for.

"Looks like our little action hero is tuckered out," Gabe whispered with a chuckle, brushing Noah's unruly curls back tenderly.

"Can you blame him? It's been quite a day," Charlotte responded, her voice filled with affection. She watched as Gabe carefully scooped Noah up into his strong arms, cradling the boy as if he weighed nothing more than a feather.

"Should we put him to bed?" Gabe asked softly, meeting her gaze with a warmth that made her heart flutter.

As he carried Noah to his bedroom, she felt a swell of emotion rise within her. She had never imagined that someone like Gabe—strong, compassionate, and deeply caring—could enter their lives and fill the void left by Noah's absent father.

Once Gabe returned to the living room, he took a seat next to her on the couch, their shoulders brushing ever so slightly. For a moment, they both stared at the screen, lost in their thoughts. Then, almost instinctively, they turned toward each other, their eyes locking in an unspoken understanding.

"Thanks for taking care of him," Charlotte said, her gratitude evident in every word. "He really looks up to you."

"Noah's a great kid, and I'm just glad I can be there for him—and you," Gabe replied, sincerity shining in his eyes.

The screen flickered, casting a soft glow across the room as Charlotte and Gabe sat side by side, their shoulders almost touching. The air was thick with anticipation, making it difficult for her to focus on the movie playing before them. Instead, she found herself stealing glances at Gabe's profile, admiring the strong lines of his jaw and the gentle curve of his lips.

As they locked eyes, the electricity between them crackled, sending shivers down Charlotte's spine. She could see the same longing in Gabe's eyes that she felt deep in her heart—a yearning for connection, for understanding, for love.

"Can I..." Gabe began, his voice thick with desire, but then he trailed off uncertainly.

"Please," Charlotte whispered, her breath catching in her throat as she leaned closer to him. The moment their lips met, it felt as though fireworks had exploded within her. The kiss was tender and sweet, yet filled with unspoken passion.

As they pulled away from each other, Charlotte looked into Gabe's eyes and saw a myriad of emotions swirling within them—hope, fear, and vulnerability. Her own heart mirrored those feelings, as she realized that she was falling for this wounded warrior who had come into her life so unexpectedly.

"Wow," Gabe breathed, his hand gently cupping her cheek. "That was..."

"Amazing," Charlotte finished for him, her eyes shining. "It's been a long time since I've felt this way about someone, Gabe."

"Me too," he admitted, his thumb tracing small circles on her cheek.

"Here's to new beginnings," she murmured, her voice little more than a whisper, barely louder than the silence surrounding them. The credits of the movie had long since scrolled off the screen.

A soft sigh escaped Charlotte's lips as she closed the space between them. Their lips met again, a soft and tender connection that spoke louder than any words ever could. It was a kiss laced with the promise of tomorrow, an assertion of a future they were willing to fight for together. The sensation was electric, shooting sparks through her every nerve, making her forget the world around her.

CHAPTER NINE

Gabe sat close beside Charlotte on the plush gray couch, their fingers intertwined. His callused thumb grazed over her soft knuckles as a comfortable silence fell between them. The familiar ache behind his eyes had dulled to a faint throb, soothed by Charlotte's presence alone.

After weeks of sleepless nights haunted by the ghosts of his past, a single evening in her company had done more to ease his troubled mind than any therapy session or prescription drug. After that first kiss, a sense of trust lingered between them, strong enough to break down barriers that had been built up over time.

"Charlotte, there's something I've been wanting to share with you."

"You can tell me anything." Her warm brown eyes encouraged him to continue.

Gabe took a deep breath, feeling the weight of the memories pressing down on his chest. "During my time in Afghanistan, I saw and experienced things that I never thought possible." His voice shook slightly, betraying the turmoil of emotions within him. "I lost friends ... people who meant the world to me."

Charlotte's gaze was unwavering, full of understanding and empathy. As Gabe looked into her warm, inviting eyes, he felt the walls he had built around his heart begin to crumble. For once, he didn't feel the need to shield himself from the world or to deny the truth of his experiences. And so he began to share.

"I was injured in an explosion on my last tour. Yes, I lost some good friends that day...but I lost a part of myself too. When I came home, everything seemed different. The world had moved on without me, and I didn't know how to fit into it anymore."

Gabe paused, searching for the right words.

"But what's really been eating away at me is this survivor's guilt. I keep asking myself why I made it back when others didn't. Why I'm still here when there are so many better men and women who didn't get that chance."

Charlotte unfolded his clenched fingers. One by one, she laid gentle kisses on his fingertips. With each kiss, Gabe fell deeper and faster into the palm of her hand.

"Your book on PTSD and soldiers, it sounds like a really important project," she said, breaking the silence. "You're going to be the one who tells their stories. You're here so that they still have a voice."

For the first time since coming home, Gabe felt the crushing weight on his chest begin to lift. Maybe, just maybe, he could leave the darkness behind and step into the light once more. As long as Charlotte was by his side, he knew he could face any demon that dared haunt his dreams.

"I don't deserve you," he rasped, emotion choking his voice.

Charlotte lifted her head to gaze up at him, her brown eyes shining with affection. "Well, that's too bad. Because I know for a fact that I deserve you."

That brought an unexpected chuckle out of him.

"I've worked so hard," she continued. "I've overcome so much. I deserve a ray of sunshine in my life. Noah, too. And I think that's you."

There had been a fortress around Gabe's heart for far too long. Tonight, with just a few words, Charlotte had rendered the imposing structure to rubble.

Gabe cupped her cheek, overwhelmed by the love and acceptance pouring from her heart. "You've given me more than I ever dreamed I could have again."

He leaned down as Charlotte tilted her head back to meet him halfway. Their lips touched in a soft, tender kiss that held the promise of a new foundation. A foundation built together that would last forever.

Just as their lips were about to meet a second time, a loud crash echoed through the house, startling them both. Gabe jumped to his feet, his body tensed as he prepared to confront whatever threat awaited them beyond the living room.

The dark figure of Charlotte's ex darkened the entryway. Tom's eyes were wild and his chest heaving. In his hands was a gun, the muzzle pointed straight at them. "What's going on here?"

Gabe's pulse raced, but he refused to back down. "Leave now, or I'll call the police."

"The police?" Tom let out a harsh laugh. "I own the police in this town. No one's going to help you." His gaze flickered to Charlotte, who cowered behind Gabe. "I won't let you take what's mine."

"Charlotte doesn't belong to you," Gabe said through gritted teeth. "If you don't leave right now, I'm going to make you regret it."

Tom's finger tightened on the trigger. "You have no idea who you're dealing with."

Gabe stood firm as the gun wavered in Tom's grip. He had stared down the barrel of a gun too many times to feel fear now. Gabe would do whatever it took to keep Charlotte and Noah safe.

"You'll never have her. Do you hear me? She's mine!" Tom took a menacing step forward.

Gabe braced himself, ready to spring into action. No one was taking Charlotte away from him. Not now, not ever.

"Step aside, *hero*. I'm here to talk to my wife."

"Ex-wife," Charlotte corrected, her voice trembling but firm as she emerged from behind Gabe.

"Semantics," Tom scoffed, his eyes never leaving Gabe. "Now move," he barked, gesturing with the gun.

"Over my dead body," Gabe challenged, planting himself firmly between Tom and Charlotte. His mind raced, searching for a way to defuse the situation without further escalating the danger. "You've hurt Charlotte enough. You're not going to do it again."

"Enough!" Tom's face contorted with rage. He raised the gun higher, his knuckles turning white around the handle.

"Tom, stop." Charlotte clutched Gabe's arm, her fingers digging into his skin, the ghost of a tremor in her grip. And then, as if making a decision only she could comprehend, she released her hold and took a step toward the danger, toward Tom.

The world around Gabe seemed to slow down. His heart pounded against his chest, a wild drum echoing the thunderous fear roaring in his ears. He wanted to yell, to scream, to reach out and pull her back, but he was rooted to the spot, paralyzed by the sudden turn of events. His instincts, honed by years in the military, screamed at him to intervene, to disarm Tom and get Charlotte to safety. But he found himself caught in the horrifying spectacle unfolding before him.

Her body language spoke volumes. The slump of her shoulders, the bow of her head. It was a sight that evoked memories of their first meeting in the diner—her trying to hide her distress, trying to remain strong.

Anger, sharp and lethal, surged through Gabe. He wanted to obliterate the cause of her pain. He wanted to erase the threat looming over her. But he had to stay rooted, had to wait for the right moment. It would be of no consequence if a stray bullet hit him. But the thought of it hitting Charlotte was unthinkable.

"Tom, please," she said calmly, taking one and then another slow and steady step toward the danger. "For Noah's sake, if not for your own, put the gun down. You don't want it to go off and wake him up."

"Tell him to leave so we can talk." Tom motioned toward Gabe.

"All right." Charlotte stepped even closer, her eyes never leaving Tom's.

There was a grim determination in her gaze, one that made Gabe's heart clench. His every instinct was screaming at him to intervene, to snatch her from the dangerous path she was threading. Gabe was about to pounce, but instead, he watched as the woman he had fallen in love with leap forward into the arms of the man who had made her life miserable. When she did, Gabe's heart well and truly stopped.

CHAPTER TEN

"Tell him to leave so we can talk."

Charlotte's first instinct was to protect Gabe, the wounded warrior who had become so special to her and who now stood behind her, his body tense with concern. Charlotte's mind raced, trying to think of any way to keep him safe from harm.

"All right," she said to Tom.

An eerie calm washed over Charlotte. She knew exactly what she had to do. She saw it so clearly, and she had Gabe to thank for it.

Charlotte took a deep breath and another step forward. Her heart pounded in her chest, but she knew she had to remain calm for both her son's sake and her own.

As she closed the distance between herself and Tom, Charlotte recalled the self-defense techniques Gabe had taught her during their sessions in his front yard. Once within arm's reach of Tom, she made her move. Her right palm shot out, striking the wrist of Tom's gun hand, while her left hand reached for the weapon itself.

"Wha—?" Tom gasped in shock as the gun slipped from his grasp, his eyes widening in disbelief.

Charlotte felt the weight of the gun in her hands, symbolic of the power she now held over her own fate. No longer would she be a passive observer in her life. She would take control, protect her family, and fight for the love she deserved.

Tom's face contorted into a snarl. He lunged at her, attempting to grab for the gun. She sidestepped, using his momentum against him, and delivered a swift knee to his midsection. He grunted in pain and doubled over. But it wasn't enough to keep him down.

Gabe roared, finally closing the distance between them. He tackled Tom to the ground with a force that shook the room. The soldier pinned her ex beneath his superior military-trained strength.

"Stay down, Tom," Gabe warned, his voice low and dangerous. "This ends here."

As Gabe kept Tom restrained, Charlotte bent down to pick up the gun, her hands trembling slightly. She held it pointed toward the floor, her grip firm, but her thoughts raced with uncertainty. What would have happened if she hadn't acted in time? The thought of losing Gabe, or worse, Noah, sent a shiver down her spine.

"Mom, are you okay?" Noah's voice cut through her thoughts, and she looked up to see him standing in the doorway, tears streaming down his cheeks.

"Sweetie, I'm fine," she reassured him, crossing the room to wrap her arms around him protectively. "Everything's okay now."

It was the honest truth this time.

"I called the police when I heard Dad's voice," said Noah.

"You did the right thing, buddy."

"Charlotte," Gabe said softly, his eyes locked on hers. "I'm proud of you."

"Thank you," she whispered back, knowing that they had turned a corner, leaving Tom's reign of terror behind them. Together, they would find healing and redemption and build a future filled with love and hope and lots more sparring sessions in private.

As though he read her mind, Gabe grinned at her. Charlotte gave him a secret smile.

The wail of sirens reached their ears, growing louder and more urgent by the second. Gratitude flooded through Charlotte as she realized help was finally on its way. The flashing red and blue lights filtered through the windows, illuminating the tense scene within the small living room. Moments later, two uniformed officers burst through the door, their weapons drawn and ready.

"Drop the weapon, ma'am!" one officer commanded, his gaze focused on Charlotte.

"Officer, I'm not the threat here," Charlotte replied, her voice firm but trembling slightly. "My ex-husband broke into my house and threatened us with this gun."

"Step back, please," the second officer instructed, cautiously approaching the trio on the floor. As Charlotte stepped away, she watched the officer secure handcuffs around Tom's wrists and hoist him to his feet.

When they stepped outside, a familiar patrol

car pulled up in front of the house, its tires crunching on the gravel drive. The sheriff's star gleamed through the curtain of darkness. Tom's eyes lit up when he saw his friend.

Darren stepped out of the car, his tall figure backlit by the headlights, making him appear larger than life. He adjusted his hat and walked with a purposeful stride toward the house. Despite everything, Charlotte had never been able to make Darren believe the nightmare that her marriage to Tom had been. But now, she prayed that he wouldn't turn a blind eye. How could he when the evidence was so plain?

Charlotte saw Sheriff Johnson's face change. The friendly, easygoing sheriff seemed to disappear, replaced by a man with a hardened gaze and a stern jawline. His eyes widened slightly, the usually soft blues hardening into icy shards. The denial, the complacency that had shadowed his actions for so long, seemed to drain out of him.

"Tom Evans, you are under arrest for breaking and entering, assault with a deadly weapon, and attempted kidnapping," he said. "You have the right to remain silent. Anything you say can and will be used against you in a court of law. You have the right to an attorney. If you cannot afford one, one will be provided for you."

Darren said nothing to Charlotte. He only glanced her way briefly, with something that could have been remorse in his eyes, and tipped his hat.

As Tom was led away in handcuffs, Charlotte allowed herself a moment to process the enormity of what had just happened. It felt surreal, as if the weight of her past had finally been lifted from her shoulders.

Outside, Gabe was making final statements to the police officers before they left. As he stepped out onto the porch, Charlotte could see the deep concern etched into his handsome features. He walked over to her, his strong arms enveloping her and Noah in a comforting embrace.

"Tom won't be able to hurt you anymore," Gabe said firmly, his voice filled with determination. "I promise you that."

Tears welled up in her eyes as she leaned against Gabe's chest. She knew that the road ahead wouldn't be easy, facing the aftermath of Tom's reign of terror and the healing process that lay ahead. But with Gabe by her side, she felt an indomitable sense of hope and resolve.

"Thank you, Gabe," she whispered, feeling her heart swell with gratitude. "For everything."

"Charlotte," Gabe began, pulling back to look into her eyes, "you were the one who showed incredible courage today. You protected your son and yourself. And I'm grateful that I could be there to help."

As Charlotte gazed into Gabe's eyes, she realized that her own inner strength had been the key to overcoming her fears and standing up against Tom. In that moment, she understood that she had the power within herself to create a better life for her and Noah, free from the shadows of her past. She was determined to step into the light with the man holding her close by her side.

CHAPTER ELEVEN

"...*And* as the dust settled around me, I realized that the true battle had only just begun—a battle to reclaim myself from the shadows of war," Gabe read from his new book. He paused for a moment, allowing the solemn silence in the room to underscore the weight of his words.

Gabe continued reading, sharing the story of how he had overcome his survivor's guilt and found a new purpose and sense of belonging in this small town—especially through the love and support of Charlotte and Noah. The audience, too, seemed to find hope within his words, their smiles growing brighter as he recounted moments of laughter, camaraderie, and shared strength.

The applause that filled the room slowly faded, and Gabe took a deep breath as he stepped down from the podium, clutching his book to his chest. A small gathering of people lingered around him, their faces etched with admiration and gratitude. Gabe felt a mix of relief and pride wash over him, knowing that he had successfully shared his story —and, in doing so, had opened his heart to those who needed to hear it most.

"Gabe." Charlotte's gentle voice cut through the soft hum of conversation, and he looked up to see her standing beside Noah, both of them beaming at him. "That was incredible. I'm so proud of you."

"Me too, Gabe!" Noah chimed in, his eyes shining with undeniable admiration. "You're really brave, like a superhero!"

A warm smile tugged at the corners of Gabe's mouth as he knelt down to be at eye level with the young boy. "Thank you, buddy. But you know what? I couldn't have done it without you and your mom. You two are my superheroes."

Charlotte's cheeks flushed a rosy pink, and she tucked a stray strand of her loose hair behind her ear. Gabe reached out to grasp Charlotte's hand, feeling the familiar warmth and comfort it brought him.

"You've helped me heal in ways I never thought possible, and for that, I'll always be grateful."

"Hey, we're a team, right?" Noah piped up, his own small hand reaching out to join theirs. "We stick together and help each other."

"Absolutely," Gabe agreed, smiling down at the boy who had become like a son to him. "We're a team, through and through."

As the trio stood there, their hands clasped together, they formed an unbreakable bond forged by love, support, and understanding. And in that moment, Gabe knew that despite the darkness of his past, brighter days lay ahead—as long as he had Charlotte and Noah by his side.

"Ouch," Charlotte said and looked down at her hip.

"Sorry about that," Gabe said with a grin.

"What have you got in your pocket?" she asked.

"Let me show you."

Gabe tugged her with one hand. Noah tugged her with the other. Gabe had let the boy in on the secret. The kid had heard about his mother's dreams more than she'd told him, and Gabe had wanted to get it perfect. Once they reached the parking lot of the library, Charlotte came to a dead halt.

"What's this?" she breathed, her voice more air than words.

The food truck sat parked in the lot. It was more than just a grand gesture; it was his way of showing Charlotte that her dreams were valid and worth pursuing. He wanted to give her something she'd been denied for too long: independence, self-confidence, and the opportunity to flourish.

A pastel-blue paint job adorned its exterior, giving it a charming, welcoming feel. Hand-painted on the side in elegant calligraphy were the words 'Charlotte's Sweet Treats.' Below, an array of drawn pastries conjured images of her delicious creations, the vision seeming to almost emanate the delightful aroma of baked goods.

"Is this...for me?" Her voice was small, almost whisper-like, her eyes welling up with tears. She reached out a trembling hand, brushing her fingers over the painted letters of her name.

"Yeah, it's for you, Charlotte."

Gabe reached into his pocket and pulled out the keyring that had poked her in the side. On the keychain were two items. A key... and a ring.

"You can't say no to the key," said Gabe. "But you can think about the ring."

Charlotte's fingers had trembled when she

touched her name on the food truck. They were steady as a rock when they reached for the key... and the ring.

"Charlotte," Gabe began, his voice steady despite the whirlwind of emotions swirling within him. "From the moment I met you, my world changed. You've shown me the beauty of love and resilience, and I can't imagine my life without you and Noah."

He took the ring from her and held it between their hearts.

"I want to spend the rest of my life with you, Charlotte. Will you marry me?"

Tears welled in her eyes, and she flung her arms around him in answer. "Yes!"

Noah whooped with joy as the two adults embraced. The moment seemed suspended in time, a perfect tableau of the love and camaraderie that had grown between Gabe, Charlotte, and Noah.

Gabe thought back to the first time he had met Charlotte and Noah, and how their unwavering love and support had been the lifeline he needed to confront his demons and begin to heal. In turn, he had become a pillar of strength for them, helping them navigate the stormy waters of their own trials and tribulations.

As the last rays of sunlight faded into twilight, Gabe looked out toward the horizon, hope and serenity blooming within his chest. And in that moment, he knew that the sun would always rise again, bringing with it the promise of new beginnings and the healing power of love. The three of them stood together, a testament to the resilience of the human spirit, their hearts forever bound by the unbreakable ties of family and friendship.

"Can you believe how far we've come since we first met?" he asked, his voice filled with wonder.

Charlotte's warm smile grew even brighter as she looked back at him. "It's hard to imagine, isn't it? We were both so lost and broken, and now... we've built something truly beautiful together."

"I think we deserve a little celebration," said Noah. "Can we get ice cream?"

"Sounds like a plan to me," Gabe agreed, his heart swelling with affection for this makeshift family he had found. Together, the trio made their way toward the creamery down the street.

As the sun dipped below the horizon, leaving behind a brilliant tapestry of orange and pink hues, it was in that tender moment that a wounded warrior, a brave mother, and her loving son silhouetted against the dying embers of the day proved that whatever the future held, they would face it together—as a team, bound by love, support, and the shared understanding that no challenge was insurmountable when they stood up for one another.

Don't miss the next book in the Honor Valley Romances!

When battle lines blur, a wounded warrior and a career-driven woman become clear about the love they once shared.

Liam Montgomery, a former soldier dealing with PTSD, finds himself fighting the most significant battle of his life when he returns home to Honor Valley. After healing his inner demons, he yearns to reclaim the love of his life. Despite the scars of the past, he's hopeful for a second chance.

Rachel, a rising career woman, has always been

Liam's stronghold. But the separation forced by Liam's trauma has put her on a path of self-reliance and personal growth. As she grapples with her budding career and the return of the man she never stopped loving, Rachel must decide what she truly wants.

Their paths intertwine as they're forced to confront the ghosts of their past and the unspoken feelings that still linger. As they navigate through old wounds, career obstacles, and a love that refuses to fade, they discover that the battlefields have changed, but their love remains the ultimate victory.

Soldier's Triumph is a heartwarming, small town, military romance that explores the power of love, growth, and healing. With the second chance at romance trope, and a wounded hero at its core, this story will sweep you away and leave you rooting for Liam and Rachel's happily ever after.

Shanae Johnson was raised by Saturday Morning cartoons and After School Specials. She still doesn't understand why there isn't a life lesson that ties the issues of the day together just before bedtime. While she's still waiting for the meaning of it all, she writes stories to try and figure it all out. Her books are wholesome and sweet, but her are heroes are hot and heroines are full of sass!

And by the way, the E elongates the A. So it's pronounced Shan-aaaaaaaa. Perfect for a hero to call out across the moors, or up to a balcony, or to blare outside her window on a boombox. If you hear him calling her name, please send him her way!

You can sign up for Shanae's Reader Group and receive a FREE NOVELLA in this world at

https://shanaejohnson.com/ReaderGroup

ALSO BY SHANAE JOHNSON

Honor Valley Romances

Soldier's Surrender

Soldier's Promise

Soldier's Courage

Soldier's Embrace

Soldier's Protection

Soldier's Triumph

The Brides of Purple Heart

On His Bended Knee

Hand Over His Heart

Offering His Arm

His Permanent Scar

Having His Back

In Over His Head

Always On His Mind

Every Step He Takes

In His Good Hands

Light Up His Life

Strength to Stand

His Grace Under Pressure

The Rangers of Purple Heart

The Rancher takes his Convenient Bride

The Rancher takes his Best Friend's Sister

The Rancher takes his Runaway Bride

The Rancher takes his Star Crossed Love

The Rancher takes his Love at First Sight

The Rancher takes his Last Chance at Love

The Silver Star Ranch Romances

His Pledge to Honor

His Pledge to Cherish

His Pledge to Protect

His Pledge to Obey

His Pledge to Have

His Pledge to Hold

a Flying Cross Ranch Romance

His Vow to Love

His Vow to Treasure

His Vow to Adore

His Vow to Trust

His Vow to Respect

His Vow to Defend

Bronze Star Ranch Romance

His Duty to Serve